About the Book

Once, in a barnyard far from here, there lived together a rooster, a pig, a ram, a goose, and a bull. Hearing that their master planned to make a meal of them, the five ran away to the dark forest, where they lived happily all summer long.

Only Bull thought of the cold winter ahead, and when no one would help him, he built a cozy winter hut all by himself. When the snow came, Bull was snug and warm inside his little house.

Outside in the cold, the other animals were trying in vain to keep warm. Very soon, Winter Hut had its first visitors. . . .

Winter Hut is a gay and funny animal story, adapted from a Russian tale by Cynthia Jameson, author of *Catofy the Clever* and *The Clay Pot Boy,* and delightfully illustrated by Ray Cruz.

Weekly Reader Children's Book Club presents

Winter

Coward, McCann & Geoghegan, Inc.

New York

Hut

adapted from a Russian tale

by Cynthia Jameson

pictures by Ray Cruz

Especially for
PYOTR

Once upon a time
in a faraway land
there lived together
a rooster,
a pig,
a ram,
a goose,
and a bull.

Their home
was in the barnyard
of an old man and an old woman.

One day,

when Rooster was up on the roof,

he heard the couple talking.

"Wife," said the old man,
"our animals are too old to work.
But they are fat enough to eat.
Let us make a tasty feast of them."
"Good!" said the old woman.
"You kill them and I'll cook them."
When Rooster heard this,
he was frightened.
Quickly he ran to tell Pig.

"Pig! Pig!" crowed Rooster.
"The old ones are going to eat us.
Let us run away!"
Pig was very frightened
when he heard this.
He ran to look for Ram.
"Ram! Ram!" cried Pig.

"The old man and old woman
are going to eat us."
Poor Ram shook with fright.
He had to tell Goose and Bull.
"Goose! Bull!" called Ram.
"The old ones are going to eat us!
Come! Let us run and hide!"

That night
Goose climbed on Bull's back
and Rooster
perched on Ram's head.

Then they hurried off
into the deep green forest.
Pig ran behind them
as fast as he could go.

It was summer now in the forest.
The earth was warm,
and there was plenty to eat.
The runaway animals
were fat and happy.
They didn't have a care.

Somewhere near an oak stump
Wolf and Bear
were stretching lazily in the sun.
How full their bellies were
with all sorts of forest food!

Time passed quickly,
and it was fall.
Soon winter would come
and cover everything with snow.
Soon Wolf and Bear would
grow hungry
and scour the bare forest
to find their dinner.
One day
Bull went to find his friend Goose.
"Goose," said he,
"winter is almost here.
Let us build a warm winter hut."
"Build it yourself," said Goose.
"I do not need a hut
to keep me warm.

When it gets cold,

I shall flap one wing over me
and the other under me.
That's the way I'll keep warm."

So Bull went off to see Ram.
"Ram," said he,
"come help me build a hut
to keep us warm in winter."
Ram was snoozing in the sun so
Bull went closer and asked again.
"Don't bother me," said Ram.

"Can't you see that
I am wearing a nice wool coat?
It shall keep me warm
all through winter!"
And he went back to sleep.
So Bull hunted here and there
until he found Pig.
He was busy rooting up truffles.

"Brother Pig," said Bull,
"surely *you* will help me build
a hut to keep us warm in winter."
"Who, *me?*" said Pig in surprise.
"You know I don't like work!
Besides, when it gets cold,
I'll just burrow under the ground."

Well,
there was still
somebody to ask.
That was Rooster!
Bull found him
next morning
atop a tree
crowing at the sun.
"Rooster!" called Bull.
"Come help me build
a cozy winter hut."
"Not I!" crowed Rooster.
"I have already found
this warm oak tree.
I will nestle in its leaves
when winter comes."

Now there was nobody left to ask,
so Bull walked sadly away.
He started to build the winter hut
all by himself.
Day after day
he gathered branches for the walls
and thatch and moss for the roof.

The floor he made out of straw
and his bed out of leaves.
He piled stone upon stone
until a fine stove
stood in the middle of the room.

Now Bull roamed the forest.

He gathered acorns,

wild berries,

and juicy roots.

These he stored in Winter Hut.

He would eat them

during the long snowy season.

Along the walls of his hut

he piled twigs and pine cones.

These would feed the fire

in his stove.

At last

Bull's work was done.

Winter Hut was ready!

Winter arrived
and buried the forest
deep in snow.

But Bull did not mind,
for he slept
snug and warm
in front of his stove.
He did not know
that far out in the forest
Wolf and Bear
were hunting for a meal
and a warm place to sleep.
Meanwhile,
right outside Winter Hut
some other animals
were very cold indeed.

Ram was jumping and dashing
through the snow,
trying his best to get warm.
His fine wool coat
was not thick enough
to keep out winter's icy blasts.

From the high oak
came Rooster's loud squawking.
All the leaves had fallen
and left the trees bare.
Now Rooster had no warm nest
where he could hide
from the wind and snow.

Down below,
Pig was grunting sadly
as he hunted for a soft place
to burrow.
Everywhere
the ground was frozen and hard,
and Pig was growing colder
and colder.

But saddest of all
was Goose.
Her wings had frozen to her sides.
They were frozen so tightly
that she could not flap
one wing over her
or one under her
to keep warm.

Very soon
Winter Hut had its first visitors.
"Let us in! Let us in!"
cried voices outside the door.
Bull looked out his window.
Standing together in the snow
were Rooster, Pig, Ram,
and Goose!

"Go away!" shouted Bull.
"You did not help me
build Winter Hut."
"But we are c-c-cold,"
whined the animals.
"You said you could keep warm
by yourselves," called Bull.
"So now you can just stay out!"

"*Baa-a-a! Baa-a-a!*" cried Ram.
"If you don't let us in,
I'll break down your door
with my hard head.
Then the cold will get in!"

"Oink-oink! Oink-oink!"
snorted Pig.
"If you don't let us in,
I'll r-r-root a big hole
under Winter Hut
and m-m-make it fall down!"

"Cock-a-doodle-doo!
Let me in too!"
crowed Rooster.
"Or I'll claw holes in your walls
and let the wind whistle through!"

"*Gagak! Gagak!*" called Goose.
"Let us in right now,
or I'll pull your roof apart
with my strong bill.
Then the snow will come in!"

Poor Bull thought and thought.
He did not want them
to destroy his Winter Hut.
He would *have* to let them in.
Slowly Bull opened the door.
With snorts and squawks of joy
the cold animals rushed inside.

First they ate up Bull's supper
of acorns and roots.
Then they gobbled his dessert
of juicy berries.

Later
Ram stretched out
beside the stove.

Pig curled up and fell asleep
on Bull's soft bed.

Goose made herself a cozy nest
in the straw.

Rooster perched up high
on the warm chimney.

Now Bull was cold,
for they had taken
all the warm places.
He was hungry, too,
for they had eaten his supper.
How angry Bull was!
If only he could find a way
to put them out of Winter Hut!
Meanwhile,
the others were snoring happily.
At last
they had a warm place
to spend the winter!
They didn't know that
from far away

Wolf and Bear
had seen the smoke
from the chimney of Winter Hut.

"Somebody must be living
in that little house,"
snarled Wolf.
"Let us go eat him up."
"Yes," growled Bear.
"After that, *we'll* sleep
in his nice warm bed."
And so, in the dark of night

the two set out for the little hut.
When they got there,
Wolf said to Bear,
"You go in first. You're *bigger!*"
"No! Not me!" cried Bear.
"You go first. You can *see* better."
"Oh, all right," growled Wolf.
"We'll go in together!"

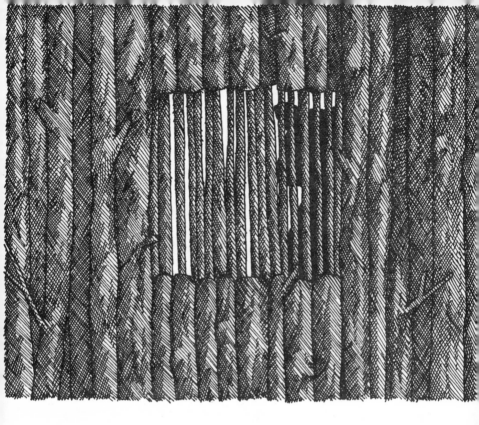

But inside Winter Hut
the barnyard animals were awake.
They could hear
Wolf and Bear
creeping up outside.
"Whatever shall we do?"
squawked Goose.

"We must attack them
all together," Bull whispered.
"Good!" agreed the others.
"We'll give them a great scare!"

Slowly . . . slowly . . .
Wolf opened the door.
Now Bear was afraid,
and he wanted to run away.
So Wolf had to push him in first.
Softly . . . softly . . .
into the hut they crept.
It was so dark inside
they could not see a thing.
All at once . . .

Bang!

    Thump!

        Swoosh-sh-sh!

        Squawk-squawk-squawk!

Bear was tossed against the wall
by Bull's horns,
bumped in the chest
by Ram's hard head.
Pig snorted and bit his soft toes.
Bull's hard hooves rapped Wolf
on the back.

He yelped and ran around the room
as Goose pulled his ears
with her bill and beat her
strong wings against his eyes.
Rooster flew down from his perch
and sank his sharp talons
into Wolf's tender nose.

And all the while
Rooster crowed loudly,
"We'll pull your ears!
We'll claw your nose!
We'll eat you up *alive!*"
Wolf's whiskers and Bear's fur
flew in all directions.
"*Ei-ei-ei-ei!* Save me!" cried Bear.
"*Ow-ow!* Let me go!" cried Wolf.

Wolf found the door.
Out he ran
into the forest.

He did not stop running
until he was far, far away.
Bear could not find the door,
so the animals pushed him out.
He ran and ran
until he found Wolf.

"Bear!" cried Wolf.
"That monster almost killed me!"
"His hard hooves
almost broke my back.
His claws cut my poor nose.
His wings blinded my eyes.
And his awful beak
almost pulled my ears off!"

"No, no!" cried Bear.
"The monster doesn't have
hooves, or claws, or wings.
He has two hard heads
and a lot of pointed horns.
And a mouth
that snorts and eats toes!"

"Well," said Wolf,
"now we know that a monster
lives in that hut.
We'll never
go back there again!"
"No," said Bear,
shaking his head, "never again!"
And so
Wolf and Bear ran far, far away.
And they never came back.

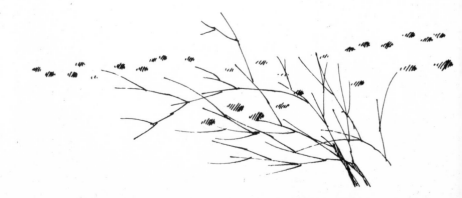

"Hee-hee-hee," giggled Pig.
"I scared them off
when I bit their toes."

"Oh, no," said Ram.
"It was my hard head
that frightened them away."

"My wings did the best job,"
squawked Goose.

"My sharp talons
hurt most of all,"
cried Rooster.

But Bull just laughed and said,
"We scared them *together*.
None of us
could have done it alone.
I am glad
we are such good friends!"
Bull, Rooster, Pig, Ram,
and Goose
laughed and laughed
about the fine joke
they had played
on Wolf and Bear.

And forever after
they lived together
warm and safe
in Winter Hut.

About the Author

WINTER HUT is Cynthia Jameson's fourth book for children. She is the author of CATOFY THE CLEVER and THE CLAY POT BOY, both published by Coward, McCann & Geoghegan, and of ONE FOR THE PRICE OF TWO. She particularly likes to draw and to write stories and poems about gypsies and animals.

About the Artist

Ray Cruz has been drawing since he was five years old. He grew up in New York City where he attended the High School of Art and Design, and studied at Pratt Institute and Cooper Union. He has done package, textile, and wall paper design as well as advertising and book illustration.

In his spare time, Ray Cruz loves to travel, especially in Italy. He is also very interested in archaeology and is an active member of several wildlife conservation groups.